HYDERABAD METRO TALES

TADI VAMSI KRISHNA

I dedicate this book to every metro passenger.

CONTENTS

Title Page

Copyright

Dedication

Preface

Prologue

On the way 1

On the way to Charminar 3

New Beginnings 5

Light in the darkness 7

How i met my Grandson 9

We're not Friends anymore 11

Fateful Bump 13

Don't be sad anyone 15

I'm nervous 17

Scared for a bit 19

One time Experience 22

Not a Good day 24

A Day to Cherish Forever 26

Sort of a dream but not 28

Mother's word 30

Emergency 32

Saviour 34

A man indeed 36

Final Verdict 38

Being Helpful 40

Time will change 42

Thief in the metro 44

Missing 46

Fake life 48

New Generation 50

In a rush 52

Ego is ? 54

Struggle 56

Tense environment 58

New relations 61

Motivation 63

Nothing can stop me 65

Duty 67

Emily 69

I am there for you 71

Father 73

Not the end	75
Good Friends	77
My Cub	79
Brother	81
Friends are not just friends	83
A help in the right time	85
Movie with a stranger	87
Zany personality	89
Passion	90
Don't be hesitant	92
Movies are not just movies	94
Grandparents are the best story tellers	96
Hyderabad metro tales	98
Memories at Charminar	100
Acknowledgement	103
About The Author	105
LETTER	107

PREFACE

Every day, many passengers travel by metro train. There is a unique story behind every passenger, whether it is a happy one or a bitter one. Sometimes we get to know other passengers' stories or share our own stories. With this idea, I came up with "Hyderabad Metro Tales". This book consists of 50 tales, sorry 50 lives. By mixing both reality and fiction, I wrote these stories. You may think about other metro passengers or you may interact with other metro passengers after you read this book. This book will make any metro passenger and reader feel the vibe of metro while reading it.

PROLOGUE

I am always looking for stories in my surroundings. While riding the metro, I began to think about the passengers. By looking at them, I visualized their stories. In the metro, every passenger is in his own head. I believe there are many unheard stories among those passengers. I created these stories by adding fiction to reality.

ON THE WAY

Once upon a time, in the bustling city of Hyderabad, two strangers met on the metro. One was a young woman named Priya, who was on her way to a job interview at a technology company. The other was a middle-aged man named Ravi, who was on his way to visit his son at college.

As they stood on the crowded train, Priya couldn't help but notice Ravi's kind face and warm smile. She struck up a conversation with him, and they quickly discovered that they had a lot in common. They both loved to read and enjoy exploring the city's many cultural attractions.

As the metro pulled into their shared stop, Priya and Ravi exchanged numbers and made plans to meet up later that week. Over the next few months, they became good friends, exploring the city and sharing many memorable experiences together.

Priya eventually landed the job at the technology company, and Ravi's son graduated from college and moved back home.

Despite the changes in their lives, they remained close friends, always grateful for the chance encounter that brought them together on the Hyderabad mero.

ON THE WAY TO CHARMINAR

It was a busy afternoon in Hyderabad, and the metro was packed with people rushing to get home or to their next destination. As the train pulled into the station, Aarav and Riya found themselves jostled and pushed by the crowds trying to board. Aarav managed to hold onto Riya's hand and they made their way onto the train, finally finding a spot to stand near the doors.

As they stood there, trying to balance as the train swayed and lurched, Aarav noticed a woman a few feet away who seemed to be struggling to hold onto a stroller with one hand and her bag with the other. Without hesitation, he stepped forward and offered to help her. The woman, whose name was Avantika, gratefully accepted and Aarav held onto the stroller while Avantika held onto her bag.

As they chatted, they discovered that they were all headed to the Charminar.

They decided to travel together and, by the time they reached their destination, they had become fast friends. They exchanged numbers and made plans to meet up the following week for lunch.

From that day on, Aarav, Riya, and Avantika became regular companions on the metro, always looking out for each other and making the daily commute a little bit brighter.

NEW BEGINNINGS

Once, on a crowded Hyderabad metro train, a man named Harsha Vardhan bumped into a woman named Veena.

"Oh, I'm so sorry," Harsha Vardhan apologized, offering Veena his hand to help steady her.

"It's okay," Veena said with a smile. "It's crowded in here."

The two struck up a conversation and discovered that they were both traveling to the same part of the city. They decided to get off at the same stop and walk to their destination together.

During the walk, Harsha Vardhan and Veena learned that they had a lot in common. They both worked in the tech industry and loved trying out new restaurants in the city.

By the time they reached their destination, they had exchanged phone numbers and made plans to meet up for dinner at a new restaurant the following weekend.

Who would have thought that a simple bump on the metro would lead to a new friendship

LIGHT IN THE DARKNESS

Rashid was a young man with a heavy heart. He had just lost his job and was struggling to make ends meet. As he rode the Hyderabad metro home from a fruitless day of job searching, he couldn't help but feel defeated.

As he sat on the crowded train, he noticed a woman a few seats away who looked just as sad as he felt. Her name was Afrin, and she too had recently lost her job.

The two strangers struck up a conversation and bonded over their shared sense of despair. They talked about their failed job searches and their fears for the future.

As they arrived at their stop, Rashid and Afrin exchanged phone numbers and promised to keep in touch.

But as the days went by, their job prospects didn't improve. Despite their best efforts, they were unable to find work and their finances only grew more dire.

Rashid and Afrin's friendship was a source of comfort in a difficult time, but it couldn't change the harsh realities of their situation. They eventually lost touch, each consumed by their own struggles.

Their brief encounter on the Hyderabad metro was a moment of connection in a sea of loneliness, but ultimately it was a fleeting one, unable to lift them out of their sadness

HOW I MET MY GRANDSON

Devi was an old woman who had never ridden the Hyderabad metro before. She lived in a small village outside the city and had always relied on her son to take her wherever she needed to go.

But today, she was determined to visit her grandson Krupakar on her own. Krupakar had just started college in the city and Devi missed him terribly.

Despite her initial nervousness, Devi managed to navigate the busy metro station and board the train with the help of a kind stranger. She clutched her bag tightly as the train began to move, taking in the sights and sounds of the city.

As she made her way to Krupakar's college, Devi couldn't help but feel a sense of pride at her accomplishment.

She had always been a bit of a homebody, but today she was venturing out on her own and it felt exhilarating.

When she finally arrived at the college, Krupakar was thrilled to see his grandmother. They spent the day touring the campus and enjoying a meal together.

As the sun began to set and it was time for Devi to catch the train back home, Krupakar walked her to the station and hugged her tightly.

"Thank you for coming to see me, Grandma," he said.

"I'm so proud of you for taking the metro all by yourself."

Devi smiled and patted her grandson's cheek. "It was scary at first," she admitted, "but it was worth it to see your face."

From that day on, Devi became a regular on the Hyderabad metro, visiting Krupakar every chance she got. She may have been an old woman, but she was full of life and adventure.

WE'RE NOT FRIENDS ANYMORE

Siddharth and Aarohi had been friends for years, but it wasn't until they met on the Hyderabad metro that they realized their feelings for each other ran much deeper.

They were both rushing to work on a crowded morning train when they found themselves standing side by side, their arms brushing against each other's.

"Sorry," Siddharth said, trying to give Aarohi some space.

But Aarohi just smiled and leaned closer to him. "It's okay," she said. "I don't mind the crowded train if it means I get to stand next to you."

Siddharth's heart skipped a beat as he realized

that Aarohi had feelings for him too. They spent the rest of the ride talking and laughing, their connection growing stronger with every passing moment.

By the time they reached their stop, they had exchanged phone numbers and made plans to go out on a proper date that weekend.

As they parted ways, Siddharth couldn't believe his luck. He had always thought of Aarohi as just a friend, but now he couldn't wait to explore their newfound feelings for each other.

Who would have thought that a crowded metro train could bring two people so close together?

FATEFUL BUMP

Samantha was running late for her train. She had been so focused on finishing up a project at work that she had lost track of time. As she rushed through the crowded Hyderabad metro station, she practically collided with a handsome stranger.

"I'm sorry," she said, feeling flustered. "I didn't see you."

"No problem," the man replied with a charming smile.

"I'm happy to have been in your way."

Samantha couldn't help but blush at the man's words. She quickly gathered her things and made her way onto the metro train, finding a seat near the back. She was disappointed to see that the man had not followed her onto the metro train.

As the train pulled away from the metro station, Samantha's thoughts turned back to her work. But as she rummaged through her bag for her laptop, she felt a tap on her shoulder.

"Excuse me, miss," the man from the metro station said, "but I think you dropped this."

Samantha's face fell as she realized that she had left her phone charger behind. "Thank you so much," she said, taking the charger from the man. "I don't know what I would have done without it."

The man chuckled. "Glad I could help. My name is Rohan, by the way."

"I'm Samantha," she replied, feeling grateful for the chance encounter.

Rohan and Samantha spent the rest of the train ride chatting and getting to know each other. By the time they reached their stop, they had exchanged phone numbers and made plans to meet up again.

From that day on, Rohan and Samantha were inseparable. They continued to ride the Hyderabad metro together, always finding new adventures and experiences in the city. And they knew that it was all thanks to that fateful bump on the crowded train.

DON'T BE SAD ANYONE

As the Secunderabad metro pulled into the station, Anika's heart was heavy with sadness. She had just received a call from her boyfriend, Roshan, who had broken up with her out of the blue. Anika couldn't understand why things had ended between them. They had been so happy just a few days before.

As she made her way to the platform, Anika's eyes filled with tears. She felt lost and alone. Suddenly, she felt a hand on her shoulder.

"Are you okay?" a kind voice asked.

Anika turned to see a man standing behind her, concern etched on his face. She couldn't help but break down in tears and tell him everything.

The man, who Introduced himself as Rohit, listened sympathetically and offered Anika a tissue. "I know it's hard to go through a breakup," he said, "but things will get better with time. You'll see."

Anika was touched by Rohit's kindness and the two spent the rest of the train ride talking and getting to know each other. By the time they reached their stop, Anika felt a little bit better. She had made a new friend who had helped to lift her spirits.

But as she said goodbye to Rohit and boarded the next train back home, Anika couldn't shake the feeling that she had missed her chance at true love. She knew that she would always remember Rohit and the kindness he had shown her on that fateful day on the Secunderabad metro

I'M NERVOUS

As the Raidurg metro pulled into the station, Shivani felt a sense of unease wash over her. She had received a mysterious text message from an unknown number earlier that day, telling her to meet at the metro station at precisely 7:00 PM.

Shivani had hesitated at first, but something about the message had piqued her curiosity. She had always been a bit of a thrill-seeker, and she couldn't resist the opportunity for a bit of excitement.

As she stepped off the train, Shivani scanned the crowded platform for any sign of the mysterious sender. She had just about given up hope when she felt a tap on her shoulder.

"Shivani," a low voice whispered in her ear. "Follow me."

Shivani's heart raced as she turned to see a hooded figure beckoning her to follow. She hesitated for a moment, but something about the figure's demeanor told her that this was not a joke.

As they made their way through the crowded station, Shivani's nerves only grew. She had no idea what she was getting herself into. But she couldn't turn back now.

The hooded figure led Shivani down a series of dark corridors, eventually coming to a stop at a locked door. Without a word, the figure produced a key and unlocked the door, gesturing for Shivani to enter.

Shivani's heart was pounding as she stepped into the dimly-lit room. She couldn't believe what she was seeing. There, sitting at a table in the center of the room, was the CEO of the company she had been trying to land a job at for months.

"I'm sorry for the cloak and dagger routine," the CEO said, standing to greet Shivani. "But I wanted to be sure I had your undivided attention. I've been impressed with your work and I'd like to offer you a job at our company."

Shivani was speechless. She had never expected her adventure on the Raidurg metro to lead to such an amazing opportunity. From that day on, she made sure to keep an open mind and never turn down a chance for excitement.

SCARED FOR A BIT

As the Ameerpet metro pulled into the station, Maya couldn't shake the feeling that something wasn't right. She had received a mysterious message from an unknown number earlier that day, inviting her to meet at the metro station at 7:00 PM.

Maya had been hesitant to come, but her curiosity had gotten the best of her. She had always been a bit of a thrill-seeker and she couldn't resist the opportunity for a bit of excitement.

As she stepped off the train, Maya scanned the crowded platform for any sign of the mysterious sender. She had just about given up hope when she felt a tap on her shoulder.

"Maya," a low voice whispered in her ear. "Follow me."

Maya's heart raced as she turned to see a hooded figure beckoning her to follow. She hesitated for a moment, but something about the figure's demeanor told her that this was not a joke.

As they made their way through the crowded

station, Maya's nerves only grew. She had no idea what she was getting herself into. But she couldn't turn back now.

The hooded figure led Maya down a series of dark corridors, eventually coming to a stop at a locked door. Without a word, the figure produced a key and unlocked the door, gesturing for Maya to enter.

Maya's heart was pounding as she stepped into the dimly-lit room. She couldn't believe what she was seeing. There, sitting at a table in the center of the room, was a group of hooded figures, their faces hidden in the shadows.

"Welcome, Maya," one of the figures said in a grave voice. "We've been watching you and we think you have what it takes to join us."

Maya's mind raced. Who were these people and what did they want from her? She knew she had to get out of there, but she was frozen with fear.

Just as she was about to make a run for it, the door burst open and a group of police officers stormed into the room. The hooded figures scattered, leaving Maya alone with the police.

As it turned out, the mysterious message had been a setup by a group of hackers who were recruiting new members. Maya had narrowly escaped becoming their latest victim.

From that day on, Maya made sure to be more careful about the invitations she accepted. She couldn't believe the danger she had narrowly avoided on the Ameerpet metro

ONE TIME EXPERIENCE

As the Lb Nagar metro pulled into the station, Kireet couldn't help but feel a sense of excitement. He had just received a message from his girlfriend, Manasa, inviting him to meet at the metro station at 7:00 PM.

Kireet had been looking forward to this moment for weeks. Manasa had been working on a surprise for him and he couldn't wait to see what it was.

As he stepped off the train, Kireet scanned the crowded platform for any sign of Manasa. He had just about given up hope when he felt a tap on his shoulder.

"Kireet," Manasa said, a huge grin on her face. "Close your eyes."

Kireet did as he was told, feeling Manasa lead him by the hand. He could feel her excitement radiating through her touch.

After a few moments, Manasa stopped and whispered, "Okay, you can open them now."

Kireet opened his eyes to see a beautiful candlelit dinner set up on the platform. There was a table with a white tablecloth, a bouquet of roses, and two place settings.

"Oh my god, Manasa," Kireet said, overwhelmed by the sight. "This is amazing."

Manasa grinned. "I wanted to do something special for us. I know we don't get to spend as much time together as we'd like, so I thought we could have a romantic dinner on the metro platform."

Kireet was touched by Manasa's thoughtfulness. They sat down at the table and enjoyed a delicious meal, surrounded by the hustle and bustle of the Lb Nagar station.

As they finished their meal and watched the trains come and go, Kireet knew that this was a moment he would always treasure. Manasa had gone above and beyond to make their time together special, and he was so grateful to have her in his life

.

NOT A GOOD DAY

It was a typical evening on the Raidurg metro as it made its way towards the Madhapur station. The train was crowded, as it always was at this time of day, but nobody could have predicted what was about to happen.

As the train pulled into the Madhapur station, a commotion broke out in the back car. Passengers rushed to see what was going on, and to their horror, they found a man lying on the ground, unresponsive.

Someone called for help and the station manager quickly arrived on the scene. He tried to revive the man, but it was too late. The man had suffered a heart attack and he was gone.

The passengers on the train were in shock. Many of them had never witnessed something like this before, and the sight of the dead man lying on the ground was traumatic.

The train was quickly evacuated and the police

were called to the scene.

The investigation revealed that the man had a history of heart problems and had not been taking his medication regularly.

As the news of the man's death spread, his family was devastated. They couldn't believe that he had died so suddenly, in such a crowded and public place.

The incident was a grim reminder of the fragility of life and the importance of taking care of one's health. It left a lasting impact on the passengers who had witnessed it, and they would never forget the tragedy that had occurred on the Raidurg metro

A DAY TO CHERISH FOREVER

As the Parade Grounds metro pulled into the station, Jagannadh and Ayesha couldn't help but feel a sense of excitement. They had been planning their wedding for months and today was finally the big day.

The couple had decided to have a small, intimate ceremony at the metro station, surrounded by a few close friends and family. They had always been a bit unconventional, and they loved the idea of starting their new life together in a unique and memorable way.

As they stepped off the train, Jagannadh and Ayesha were greeted by their loved ones, who had gathered on the platform to witness their union. The couple exchanged vows and exchanged rings, surrounded by the sounds of the busy metro station.

After the ceremony, the group celebrated with a champagne toast and a cake cutting. It was a simple but perfect celebration, filled with love and joy.

As the day came to a close and the group said their goodbyes, Jagannadh and Ayesha knew that they would always remember the special day they were married on the Parade Grounds metro. It was a day they would never forget

SORT OF A DREAM BUT NOT

Vimesh couldn't believe his luck as he boarded the Secunderabad metro. He had always been a bit of a shy guy and he had never expected anything like this to happen to him.

As he found a seat and settled in for the ride, a beautiful girl approached him. She introduced herself as Aarohi and asked if she could sit next to him. Vimesh was a little taken aback, but he couldn't resist the chance to talk to such a gorgeous woman.

The two of them struck up a conversation and Vimesh found himself completely charmed by Aarohi. She was smart, funny, and full of life. As the train ride went on, Vimesh couldn't believe how much he enjoyed her company.

Just as the train was pulling into the Secunderabad station, Aarohi leaned in and kissed Vimesh on the cheek. "Thank you for a wonderful ride," she said with a wink before disappearing into the crowds.

Vimesh was left in shock, but he couldn't wipe the smile off his face. He had just experienced the most unexpected and wonderful moment of his life on the Secunderabad metro

MOTHER'S WORD

As the Durgam Cheruvu metro pulled into the station, Biswajeet couldn't help but feel a sense of nervousness wash over him. He had an important job interview at a top company in the city, and he knew that this was his chance to make a good impression.

As he stepped off the train and made his way towards the interview location, Biswajeet couldn't help but feel a little bit intimidated. He had always been a bit of an introvert and the thought of facing a panel of interviewers made him feel anxious.

But as he walked through the crowded streets of the city, Biswajeet remembered something his mother had told him: "You are capable of achieving anything you set your mind to."

Those words gave Biswajeet the motivation he needed. He took a deep breath and reminded himself that he had worked hard and was more than qualified for this opportunity.

As he walked into the interview room, Biswajeet exuded confidence. He answered the questions with ease and impressed the panel with his knowledge and experience.

When the interview was over, Biswajeet couldn't believe how well it had gone. He knew that it was all thanks to the motivation he had found on his journey on the Durgam Cheruvu metro.

A few days later, Biswajeet received the good news that he had been offered the job. He couldn't wait to start his new career and he knew that he had the Durgam Cheruvu metro to thank for the push he needed to succeed

EMERGENCY

As the metro whizzed through the city, the passengers on board had no idea of the danger they were in. Everything seemed normal until the driver, Mr. Sharma, slumped over the steering wheel with a heart attack.

Panic broke out on the train as passengers realized what had happened. They tried to revive Mr. Sharma, but it was too late. He was gone.

With no one to control the speeding train, the passengers knew that their lives were in grave danger. They frantically tried to come up with a plan to stop the train before it was too late.

One passenger, a young man named Mohit, knew that he had to take action. He had always been fascinated by trains and he knew a little bit about how they worked.

Rohit quickly assessed the situation and realized that the only way to stop the train was to manually activate the emergency brakes. He knew it was a risky move, but he also knew that it was the only hope they had.

Without hesitation, Mohit raced to the front of the train and activated the brakes. There was a loud screeching sound as the train came to a halt, sending passengers flying forward.

When the dust settled, Mohit found himself surrounded by grateful passengers, who were thanking him for his quick thinking and bravery. Mohit was overwhelmed by their gratitude, but he knew that he had only done what needed to be done to save their lives.

As the passengers waited for help to arrive, they couldn't help but think about the tragedy that had befallen them on the metro. It was a harsh reminder of the fragility of life and the importance of being prepared for the unexpected

SAVIOUR

There was a doctor named Maria who worked at a hospital in the city. One day, she received a call from the emergency department informing her that a patient was on their way to the hospital by metro. The patient was experiencing severe chest pain and needed to be treated as soon as possible.

Maria knew that every minute counted in this situation, so she quickly grabbed her bag and headed out of the hospital. She hailed a taxi and rushed to the nearest metro station. She arrived at the station just in time to see the metro pulling into the platform.

Without hesitation, Maria boarded the train and made her way to the patient. She found the patient, who was sweating and clutching their chest in pain, and immediately began to assess their condition. Maria realized that the patient was experiencing a heart attack and needed to get to the hospital as soon as possible.

She instructed the patient to remain calm and

tried to reassure them that everything would be alright.

Maria then contacted the hospital and informed them of the situation, requesting that a team be ready to receive the patient as soon as they arrived.

The metro arrived at the hospital a few minutes later, and Maria and the patient were met by the hospital team. The patient was rushed to the emergency department and received the necessary treatment. Thanks to Maria's quick actions and expertise, the patient made a full recovery. Maria was grateful to have been able to help save a life and was proud of the work that she did as a doctor.

A MAN INDEED

There was an old man named Ranga rao who lived in a small town. He had always been a kind and generous person, always willing to lend a helping hand to those in need. One day, Ranga rao heard about a young girl named Sophia who was in desperate need of an organ transplant. Sophia had been diagnosed with a rare medical condition and needed a new liver in order to survive.

Ranga rao knew that he could not sit by and do nothing while Sophia suffered. He made the decision to donate one of his own organs to save her life. Despite being in his seventies, Ranga rao was in good health and felt that he had a lot of life left to give.

The hospital that Sophia was being treated at was located in the city, and Ranga rao lived in a small town a few hours away. He knew that he needed to get to the hospital as quickly as possible in order to be evaluated as a donor.

Ranga rao packed a bag and headed to the metro

station, determined to do everything he could to help Sophia.

He rode the metro to the city, staring out the window at the passing scenery as he thought about the young girl he was trying to save.

As the metro approached the city, Ranga rao's thoughts turned to the surgery that lay ahead. He knew that it would be a risky procedure, but he was determined to do everything he could to help Sophia.

When Ranga rao arrived at the hospital, he was met by the transplant team who had been waiting for him. He underwent the necessary medical tests and it was determined that he was a suitable donor for Sophia. The transplant surgery was scheduled for the following day.

The surgery was a success and Sophia received the life-saving liver transplant that she needed. Ranga rao recovered well and was proud to have been able to help save Sophia's life. He remained close with Sophia and her family, and would often visit them to check on her progress. Sophia went on to make a full recovery and live a healthy, happy life thanks to Ranga rao's selfless act of kindness.

FINAL VERDICT

There was a lawyer named Rachel who worked at a law firm in the city. She was known for her fierce determination and her ability to always get the job done, no matter how difficult the case.

One day, Rachel received a call from the Court informing her that the final verdict in a divorce case that she had been working on was going to be announced that morning. Rachel knew that this was a crucial moment in the case and that it was her responsibility to be there to represent her client.

She quickly gathered her things and headed to the metro station, determined to get to the Court on time. As she rode the metro, Rachel went over the details of the case in her mind, trying to anticipate any questions or objections that the judge might have.

When Rachel arrived at the Court, she made her way to the courtroom and took her seat at the counsel table. The judge entered the room and the proceedings began. Rachel stood up and presented her arguments, making a strong case for her client.

After listening to both sides, the judge announced the final verdict. Rachel's client was granted the divorce, and Rachel was relieved that her hard work had paid off. She left the Court feeling satisfied and proud of the work that she had done.

BEING HELPFUL

There was a young boy named Tarun who lived in the city with his family. Tarun was known for his kind and compassionate nature, always willing to help others in need.

One day, while riding the metro to visit his grandparents, Tarun noticed an old woman struggling to carry her heavy bags off the train. The woman was struggling to hold onto the bags and the railing at the same time, and it was clear that she was having a difficult time.

Without hesitation, Tarun rushed over to the woman and offered to help her with her bags. The woman gratefully accepted his offer and allowed Tarun to take one of the bags from her. Together, they made their way off the train and onto the platform.

As they walked, the woman thanked Tarun for his kind act and told him what a gentleman he was. Tarun blushed with pride and told the woman that it was his pleasure to help her.

When they arrived at the woman's destination, Tarun insisted on carrying both of the woman's bags to her destination. The woman was touched by Tarun's kindness and thanked him again before heading off.

Tarun returned home feeling proud of himself for having been able to help someone in need. He knew that it was the small acts of kindness that made a big difference in the world, and he was determined to continue helping others whenever he could.

TIME WILL CHANGE

It was a dark and stormy night, and the metro station was all but deserted. The only people there were a few stragglers waiting for the last train of the night, huddled under the awning to escape the pouring rain.

Suddenly, a figure emerged from the shadows. It was a man, his face contorted with fear and desperation. He was drenched from head to toe, and it was clear that he had been running for a long time.

As he approached the group of people, they could see that he was wearing a prison jumpsuit. It was immediately clear that he was an escaped prisoner.

The group of people tried to back away, but the man was too fast. He grabbed one of them, a young woman, and held a knife to her throat.

"I need your help," he said, panting heavily. "I

need to get out of here. I need a place to hide."

The group was terrified, but they knew they had to do something. They managed to calm the man down and convinced him to release the young woman. They then worked together to come up with a plan to help the man escape the city and start a new life.

Thanks to their quick thinking and bravery, the escaped prisoner was able to evade capture and begin a new, law-abiding life. And the group of people who had helped him would always remember the night they encountered an escaped prisoner at the metro station.

THIEF IN THE METRO

It was a crowded day at the metro station, with people rushing to and fro to catch their metro trains. Among them was a young man named Dhanush, who was known for his quick hands and ability to steal without being noticed.

Dhanush scanned the crowd, looking for his next target. He spotted an older woman with a purse that looked easy to snatch. Dhanush moved in closer, using the crowded platform to his advantage.

Just as Dhanush was about to make his move, a hand reached out and grabbed his arm. It was a police officer, who had been watching Dhanush's movements closely.

"I think you'll be coming with me," the officer said sternly.

Dhanush tried to protest, but it was no use. He was taken into custody and charged with theft.

As he sat in his cell, Dhanush couldn't help but think about how close he had come to getting away with another crime. He vowed to turn his life around and never steal again, knowing that it was only a matter of time before he was caught again.

MISSING

It was a busy day at the metro station, with people rushing to and fro to catch their trains. Among them was a young girl named Nayra, who had gotten separated from her family.

Nayra was only five years old and was starting to get scared. She didn't know where her parents were or how to get back to them. She started to cry, hoping that someone would notice her and help her.

As luck would have it, a kind-hearted woman named Sarah saw Nayra and immediately knew that something was wrong. She went over to the little girl and asked if she was lost.

Nayra nodded her head, tears streaming down her face. Sarah comforted the girl and asked her if she knew her parents' names or how to reach them.

Nayra told Sarah that her parents' names were John and Mary, and that they had been on their way to the airport. Sarah quickly pulled out her phone and called the airport, hoping to find Nayra's parents.

After a few minutes of searching, Sarah was able to locate John and Mary. She explained the situation to them and promised to stay with Nayra until they could get back to the metro station.

When John and Mary arrived, they were relieved to find Nayra safe and sound. They thanked Sarah profusely and promised to be more careful in the future. Sarah was happy to have been able to help reunite the family and went on her way, feeling grateful to have been able to make a difference in Nayra's life.

FAKE LIFE

There was a politician named Rajappa who had recently been elected to office. Rajappa was known for his smooth talk and charisma, but many people suspected that he was more concerned with his own interests than those of his constituents.

One day, Rajappa was riding the metro to a campaign event when he overheard a group of passengers discussing him. The passengers were criticizing Rajappa for his fake act and for not truly caring about the issues that mattered to them.

Rajappa was taken aback by the criticism and felt hurt and angry. He had always tried to present himself as a sincere and dedicated public servant, and it was difficult for him to hear that others did not see him that way.

Despite his feelings, Rajappa knew that he had to keep up appearances. He forced a smile and tried to engage the passengers in conversation, hoping to win them over with his charm.

But the passengers were not easily swayed. They

saw through Rajappa's act and continued to criticize him, much to his dismay.

Rajappa left the metro feeling shaken and defeated. He knew that he needed to do better if he wanted to earn the trust and respect of the people he represented. He resolved to listen more closely to their concerns and to be more transparent and genuine in his dealings with them.

NEW GENERATION

There was a CEO named Prachi who ran a successful tech company. Prachi was always on the lookout for talented individuals to join her team, and she was particularly interested in finding young, up-and-coming professionals who could bring fresh ideas and energy to the company.

One day, Prachi decided to take the metro to a local university in the hopes of finding some talented students to recruit. She packed a bag with informational flyers and business cards and headed to the metro station.

As Prachi rode the metro, she kept an eye out for anyone who looked particularly bright or ambitious. She struck up conversations with several students, asking them about their interests and career goals.

Prachi was pleased to find that there were many talented and driven students at the university, and she was able to recruit several of them to join her company. She returned to the office feeling excited about the new additions to her team and confident that they would be a valuable asset to the company.

IN A RUSH

There was a businessman named David who was on his way to an important meeting. He had spent the last few weeks preparing for the meeting and was feeling confident and ready to present his ideas.

As David rode the metro, he pulled out his laptop to review his notes one last time. But as he was scrolling through the document, a person accidentally hit David then David's laptop slipped out of his hands and fell to the floor.

David's heart sank as he saw his laptop tumble down the aisle. He quickly grabbed his bag and chased after it, but it was too late. The laptop had fallen through the open doors of the train and onto the tracks below.

David was devastated. He knew that his laptop contained all of the information he needed for the meeting, and he had no backup copies. He frantically tried to retrieve the laptop, but it was too risky to go down onto the tracks.

Feeling defeated, David returned to his seat and tried to come up with a plan. He knew that he had to find a way to retrieve his laptop and get to the meeting on time, or his career could be in jeopardy.

Just as David was starting to panic, a kind-hearted passenger offered to help. The passenger had a laptop with them and offered to let David use it for the meeting.

David was grateful for the offer and quickly transferred all of his files to the passenger's laptop. He then made his way to the meeting, determined to make the best of the situation.

In the end, the meeting was a success and David was able to present his ideas without a hitch. He was grateful to the passenger who had helped

EGO IS ?

There was a young woman named Mia who was known for her strong personality and ego. She was confident and self-assured, and she always believed that she was right.

One day, Mia was riding the metro when she saw an old man sitting across from her. The old man was reading a book and seemed completely immersed in it, completely unaware of his surroundings.

Mia couldn't help but feel annoyed by the old man's lack of awareness. She decided to teach him a lesson and started loudly talking on her phone, using exaggerated hand gestures and speaking in a loud, aggressive tone.

The old man looked up from his book and gave Mia a gentle smile. Mia was taken aback by the old man's calm demeanor and realized that she had been acting childish.

Feeling embarrassed, Mia apologized to the old man and asked him about his book. The old man told her about the book, a mystery novel, and the two struck up a conversation.

As they talked, Mia realized that the old man was actually quite intelligent and had a lot of interesting things to say. She began to see him in a new light and was grateful for the opportunity to learn from him.

Mia left the metro feeling humbled and grateful for the encounter with the old man. She learned that it was important to listen to others and to be open

STRUGGLE

Once upon a time, there was an upcoming actor named Jack who was working hard to make a name for himself in the entertainment industry. Despite facing numerous setbacks and rejections, Jack never gave up on his dream and continued to audition for various roles.

One day, while commuting to an audition via the metro, Jack met a young scientist named Sarah. Sarah was a genius in her field and had already made significant contributions to science at a young age. Despite her busy schedule, she always made time to take the metro as she enjoyed the solitude it provided her to think and work on her research.

As Jack and Sarah struck up a conversation, they discovered that they had a lot in common. Both of them were passionate about their respective fields and were determined to succeed. They also shared a love for reading and discussing ideas.

As they continued to meet and talk during their daily commute, their friendship deepened and they became good friends.

Jack was inspired by Sarah's intelligence and hard work, and Sarah was impressed by Jack's dedication and perseverance in pursuing his acting career.

Eventually, their friendship led to a romantic relationship and they decided to move in together. Sarah's genius mind and Jack's creative talent made for a perfect match and they supported each other in their respective careers.

Thanks to their mutual support and encouragement, Jack's acting career took off and he landed some major roles, while Sarah's research garnered international recognition. They were a perfect match and lived happily ever after.

TENSE ENVIRONMENT

It was a normal weekday morning and the metro was packed with commuters on their way to work. Among them was a man named Ahmed, who was on his way to carry out a terrorist attack. He had been planning this attack for months and was determined to see it through.

As he sat on the crowded Metro train, Ahmed's gaze fell on a young woman seated across from him. She was engrossed in a book and seemed completely unaware of her surroundings. Ahmed couldn't help but feel drawn to her and found himself unable to look away.

The woman, whose name was Shaheen Begum, was a police officer on her way to work. Like Ahmed, she was focused on her job and had no idea that the man seated across from her was a terrorist.

As the Metro train journeyed on, Ahmed and

Shaheen Begum struck up a conversation.

Ahmed was surprised to find that Shaheen Begum was kind and intelligent, and he found himself enjoying their conversation. Shaheen Begum, on the other hand, was intrigued by Ahmed's passion and determination, and was happy to have made a new friend.

As the Metro train neared their stop, Ahmed and Shaheen Begum said their goodbyes and went their separate ways. Little did they know that their paths would soon cross again, and in a very different context.

A few hours later, Ahmed carried out his terrorist attack and was quickly apprehended by the police. As he was being led away in handcuffs, he was shocked to see Shaheen Begum among the officers arresting him.

The two of them locked eyes and Ahmed knew in that moment that he had made a mistake. Shaheen Begum, on the other hand, was filled with sadness as she realized the true nature of the man she had just spent the morning talking to.

Despite the circumstances of their meeting, Ahmed and Shaheen Begum's encounter had a lasting impact on both of them. Ahmed learned the value of empathy and understanding, and Shaheen Begum learned that everyone, no matter their background or beliefs, is worthy of compassion.

NEW RELATIONS

There was once an old woman named Mrs. Krishna who lived alone in a small apartment. Despite her advanced age, Mrs. Krishna was fiercely independent and loved nothing more than taking the metro to the city to do some shopping or visit the local library.

One day, while waiting for the train at the station, Mrs. Krishna noticed an elderly gentleman standing nearby. He seemed a bit lost and was fumbling with a map, trying to figure out where he was going.

Feeling sorry for the man, Mrs. Krishna decided to approach him and offer her assistance. The man, whose name was Mr. Pratap, gratefully accepted her help and the two of them struck up a conversation as they waited for the train.

As they rode the metro together, Mrs. Krishna and Mr. Pratap discovered that they had a lot in common. Both of them were retired and loved spending their days exploring the city and learning new things. They also shared a love of reading and had similar tastes in books.

Over the course of their journey, Mrs. Krishna and Mr. Pratap became fast friends and decided to make a regular habit of taking the metro together. They enjoyed each other's company and looked forward to their daily trips on the train.

As the weeks and months went by, Mrs. Krishna and Mr. Pratap became like family to each other. They supported and cared for each other and their friendship brought joy and meaning to their lives.

Despite their advanced age, Mrs. Krishna and Mr. Pratap remained active and engaged in the world around them, and their bond grew stronger with each passing day.

MOTIVATION

There was once a young boy named Stephen who lived in a group home for orphaned children. Despite his difficult circumstances, Stephen was a bright and determined child who never let his circumstances get him down.

One day, while riding the metro to school, Stephen noticed a well-dressed man seated across from him. The man was engrossed in a book and seemed completely unaware of his surroundings. Stephen couldn't help but feel drawn to the man and his love of reading, and found himself wanting to know more about him.

As the train journeyed on, Stephen mustered up the courage to approach the man and strike up a conversation. To his surprise, the man was friendly and welcoming, and the two of them had a great conversation about books and ideas.

As they talked, Stephen learned that the man was a successful businessman who had worked hard to achieve his success.

The man was impressed by Stephen's curiosity and determination, and offered to mentor him and help him achieve his own dreams.

Over the course of their relationship, the man, whose name was Mr. Thompson, became a role model and mentor for Stephen. He taught Stephen valuable lessons about hard work, perseverance, and the importance of education.

Thanks to Mr. Thompson's guidance and support, Stephen excelled in school and eventually went on to attend college. He never forgot the impact that Mr. Thompson had on his life and remained grateful to him for the rest of his days.

Stephen's story is a reminder that no matter where we come from or what challenges we face, we all have the potential to achieve greatness with the right guidance and support.

NOTHING CAN STOP ME

There was once a young dancer named Pratima who was preparing for the finals of a prestigious dance competition. She had been practicing for months and was determined to give it her all on stage.

On the day of the finals, Pratima was running late and rushed to catch the metro to the venue. As she was rushing to board the train, she tripped and fell, twisting her ankle in the process.

Panicked and in pain, Pratima couldn't believe her luck. The finals were in just two hours and she was unable to walk, let alone dance.

As she sat on the floor of the station, feeling helpless and defeated, a kind stranger approached her and offered to help. The stranger, whose name was Alex, was a doctor and offered to take a look at Pratima's ankle.

After examining her injury, Alex determined that Pratima had sprained her ankle and would need to rest it in order to recover. Despite her disappointment, Pratima knew that Alex was right and reluctantly agreed to sit out the finals.

As they waited for the next train, Alex and Pratima struck up a conversation and discovered that they shared a love of dance. Alex, it turned out, was a former dancer who had retired from the stage due to an injury.

As they talked, Alex encouraged Pratima to never give up on her dreams and to always pursue her passions. He told her that setbacks and challenges were a natural part of life and that the important thing was to never let them defeat her.

Pratima was touched by Alex's words and his kindness and was grateful to have met him. Despite not being able to participate in the finals, Pratima left the metro station feeling inspired and determined to come back stronger than ever.

DUTY

There was once a young man named Revanth who lived in the city and made a living as a thug. Despite his intelligence and potential, Revanth had become caught up in a life of crime and was constantly in and out of trouble with the law.

One day, while riding the metro to carry out a robbery, Revanth noticed a police officer seated across from him. The officer, whose name was John, was a seasoned veteran of the force but was currently on desk duty due to a leg injury.

As Revanth watched John struggle to stand up and get off the train at his stop, he couldn't help but feel a twinge of guilt. Despite their differences, Revanth and John were both intelligent and capable men who had ended up on opposite sides of the law.

As he watched John walk away, Revanth made a decision. He knew that he had the potential to turn his life around and make a positive impact on the world. He also knew that it wouldn't be easy, but he was determined to try.

Over the next few months, Revanth worked hard to turn his life around. He sought help from a mentor and began to focus on his education and his future. He also made a point of avoiding the metro, as he knew that it was a place where he was likely to encounter temptation.

Eventually, Revanth's hard work paid off and he landed a job at a tech company. He was grateful for the second chance he had been given and was determined to make the most of it.

As for John, he eventually recovered from his injury and returned to the force. Despite their rocky start, Revanth and John eventually formed a respectful and mutually beneficial relationship, with Revanth using his connections and intelligence to help John solve cases and John using his position to help Revanth stay out of trouble.

EMILY

There was once a writer named Emily who spent her days commuting to and from the city on the metro. Emily loved the solitude and quiet of the train, as it provided her with the perfect space to work on her writing.

One day, while riding the metro, Emily struck up a conversation with a fellow passenger. The passenger, whose name was Dave, was a retired librarian and an avid reader. Dave and Emily quickly discovered that they had a shared love of literature and spent the entire ride talking about their favorite books and authors.

As their conversation continued, Emily confided in Dave that she was struggling to find her voice as a writer. Despite her talent, she had a hard time believing in herself and was constantly plagued by self-doubt.

Dave listened sympathetically and offered Emily some words of encouragement. He told her that every great writer had faced setbacks and struggles, but that it was important to keep writing and to never give up on her dreams.

Emily was touched by Dave's kindness and wisdom, and was grateful to have met him. She took his advice to heart and continued to write, eventually finding her voice and becoming a successful author.

From then on, Emily made a point of striking up conversations with her fellow passengers on the metro. She met all sorts of interesting people and learned from their experiences and perspectives. And she always remembered the wise words of Dave, the retired librarian who had helped her find her way as a writer.

I AM THERE
FOR YOU

There was once an artist named Spandana who loved nothing more than drawing the world around her. She was especially drawn to the vibrant and ever-changing views of the city as seen from the metro.

One day, while riding the metro to her studio, Spandana pulled out her sketchbook and pencils and began to draw the view outside the window. As she worked, she noticed a young boy seated across from her, watching her intently.

The boy, whose name was Siva, was fascinated by Spandana's art and asked if he could watch her draw. Spandana, who enjoyed sharing her passion with others, happily agreed and allowed Siva to watch over her shoulder as she worked.

As they spent time together on the metro, Spandana and Siva became friends.

Siva was fascinated by Spandana's talent and asked her all sorts of questions about her art and her process. Spandana, in turn, was inspired by Siva's curiosity and enthusiasm, and was happy to share her knowledge with him.

Eventually, their conversations turned to Siva's own interests and dreams. It turned out that Siva was a talented musician and was struggling to find the confidence to pursue his passion.

Spandana encouraged Siva to follow his dreams and to never let fear or self-doubt hold him back. She told him that with hard work and perseverance, he could achieve anything he set his mind to.

Siva was touched by Spandana's words and took her advice to heart. He began to practice and perform more regularly, and eventually landed a spot in a local youth orchestra.

Spandana and Siva remained friends and continued to inspire each other in their respective fields. And every time they rode the metro together, they would sit and chat, sharing their passions and dreams with each other.

FATHER

There was once a father named Peter who was feeling particularly unhappy as he rode the metro home from work. He had forgotten his son's birthday and had nothing to give him when he arrived home.

As Peter sat on the train, feeling guilty and defeated, a kind stranger seated next to him struck up a conversation. The stranger, whose name was Mary, was a retired schoolteacher and could tell that Peter was feeling down.

Mary asked Peter what was troubling him and he confided in her about his forgetfulness and his fear of disappointing his son. Mary listened sympathetically and offered Peter some words of encouragement. She told him that it wasn't the gift itself that mattered, but the love and thought behind it.

Peter was touched by Mary's kindness and wisdom and decided to follow her advice. When he arrived home, he apologized to his son for forgetting his birthday and promised to make it up to him in the future.

To Peter's surprise, his son was understanding and forgiving, and was just happy to have his father home with him. The two of them spent the evening together, playing games and having a great time.

From then on, Peter made a point of being more present and attentive in his son's life, and their relationship grew stronger as a result. And every time he rode the metro, Peter thought back to the kind words of Mary, the retired schoolteacher who had helped him see the importance of love and connection.

NOT THE END

There was once a young woman named Samyuktha who was struggling with feelings of hopelessness and despair. She was unmarried and felt that she had failed to live up to the expectations of her family and society.

One day, while riding the metro to the city, Samyuktha made the decision to end her life. She planned to jump in front of the train at the next stop and end her suffering once and for all.

As the train approached the stop, Samyuktha stood up and prepared to make her move. But at the last moment, a kind stranger seated next to her reached out and grabbed her hand.

The stranger, whose name was Sramyuja, was a retired therapist and had noticed that Samyuktha was upset. She asked Samyuktha if she was okay and offered to listen if she needed to talk.

Samyuktha was hesitant at first, but eventually confided in Sramyuja about her feelings of hopelessness and her plans to end her life.

Sramyuja listened patiently and offered Samyuktha words of encouragement and hope. She told Samyuktha that she was not alone and that there was always a way forward, no matter how difficult things seemed.

Samyuktha was touched by Sramyuja's kindness and the sincerity of her words. She began to see that there might be another way forward and decided to seek help for her mental health.

Thanks to Sramyuja's intervention, Samyuktha was able to get the support she needed and eventually found happiness and fulfillment in her life. And every time she rode the metro, she thought back to the kind stranger who had saved her life and helped her see the value in hers.

GOOD FRIENDS

There was once a man named Lokesh who was known for his negative attitude and pessimistic outlook on life. Despite his intelligence and potential, Lokesh was always quick to focus on the negative and saw the glass as half empty rather than half full.

One day, while riding the metro to work, Lokesh found himself seated next to a woman named Himaja. Himaja was known for her positive attitude and upbeat personality, and was always looking on the bright side of things.

As they rode the train together, Lokesh couldn't help but be drawn in by Himaja's optimistic outlook. Despite his initial resistance, he found himself opening up to her and sharing his thoughts and feelings.

Himaja listened patiently and offered Lokesh words of encouragement and hope. She told him that it was important to focus on the good things in life and to never let negativity hold him back.

Over the course of their journey, Lokesh began to see the world in a different light.

He started to focus on the positive aspects of his life and learned to see the glass as half full rather than half empty.

As for Himaja, she was glad to have had the opportunity to help Lokesh see the world in a different way. She knew that it wasn't easy to change one's perspective, but was glad to have made a positive impact on someone's life.

From then on, Lokesh and Himaja became good friends and continued to inspire and support each other. And every time they rode the metro together, they reminded each other of the importance of a positive attitude and the power it has to change our lives.

MY CUB

There was once a zoo keeper named Kishore who was responsible for caring for a group of tiger cubs at the city's zoo. Kishore loved his job and took great pride in the care he provided for the animals under his charge.

One day, while transporting a young tiger cub named Simba to a vet appointment via the metro, disaster struck. As they were transferring trains, Kishore momentarily turned his back on Simba's carrier and the cub managed to escape.

Panicked and heartbroken, Kishore searched the station and the surrounding area for Simba, but to no avail. He knew that it was only a matter of time before someone spotted the cub and called the authorities, and he was determined to find him before it was too late.

As he rode the metro, trying to come up with a plan, Kishore noticed a young girl seated across from him. The girl, whose name was Soumya, was watching him with a curious expression on her face.

Kishore couldn't help but feel drawn to Soumya and decided to confide in her about his predicament. Soumya listened sympathetically and offered to help Kishore search for Simba.

Together, Kishore and Soumya rode the metro and scoured the city, determined to find Simba and bring him home safely. Eventually, after many hours of searching, they spotted the cub curled up in a flowerbed in a park.

Overjoyed and relieved, Kishore scooped up Simba and thanked Soumya for her help. Soumya, in turn, was happy to have played a role in reuniting Kishore and Simba

BROTHER

There was once a pair of cousin brothers named Mohan and Vinod who lived in the same neighborhood and enjoyed spending time together. One day, while riding the metro to the city to go shopping, Mohan and Vinod struck up a conversation about their family.

As they talked, they reminisced about their childhood and the memories they had shared together. They laughed about the silly pranks they used to play on each other and the adventures they had gone on.

As the train journeyed on, Mohan and Vinod realized that they had grown closer over the years and had developed a deep bond of friendship. They were grateful to have each other and vowed to make the most of the time they had together.

As they arrived at their destination, Mohan and Vinod made a plan to spend the day exploring the city and trying new things. They spent the day shopping, visiting museums, and trying new foods, all the while enjoying each other's company and the memories they were making.

As they rode the metro home that evening, Mohan and Vinod felt grateful and happy. They knew that they were lucky to have each other and that their bond was something special. And they made a promise to always make time for each other and to continue creating new memories together.

FRIENDS ARE NOT JUST FRIENDS

There was once a group of friends named Manikanta, Eswar, and Viswanth who were passionate about cricket and spent their free time playing and watching the sport. One day, while riding the metro to a big cricket match, they received some terrible news.

Their friend, who was also a member of their cricket team, had been hospitalized with a serious illness and was in need of costly medical treatment. The group was devastated by the news and were at a loss for what to do.

As they rode the metro, they began to discuss their options. They knew that they needed to come up with a plan to raise the money for their friend's treatment, and quickly.

It was then that Viswanth had an idea. He remembered that the winner of the upcoming cricket match would receive a large cash prize, and suggested that they use the prize money to help their friend.

The group was hesitant at first, as they knew that the competition was fierce and the odds were against them. But they were also determined to do whatever it took to help their friend, and eventually decided to go through with the plan.

Despite their nerves and doubts, the group played their hearts out and eventually emerged as the winners of the match. They were overjoyed by their victory and couldn't wait to use the prize money to help their friend.

Thanks to their hard work and determination, the group was able to raise the funds needed for their friend's medical treatment. And as they rode the metro home that evening, they were filled with gratitude and pride, knowing that they had done everything in their power to help their friend in need.

A HELP IN THE RIGHT TIME

There was once a man named Varun who was struggling with his health. Despite his best efforts, he had been unable to shake a persistent cough and had lost a significant amount of weight as a result.

One day, while riding the metro to work, Varun found himself seated next to a woman named Lily. Lily was a nurse and noticed that Varun was looking unwell. She asked if he was okay and offered to take a look at his cough.

Varun was hesitant at first, but eventually agreed. Lily examined Varun and determined that he was suffering from a severe case of bronchitis. She prescribed him some medicine and gave him some advice on how to take care of himself.

Varun was grateful for Lily's help and began to follow her advice.
He took his medicine as directed and made an

effort to eat healthier and get more rest. Slowly but surely, his health began to improve.

As Varun rode the metro to work each day, he thought back to the kind stranger who had helped him get on the road to recovery. He knew that he had Lily to thank for his improved health and was grateful to have met her.

MOVIE WITH A STRANGER

There was once a man named Vikas who was known for his laid-back and easy-going personality. He enjoyed meeting new people and trying new things, and was always up for an adventure.

One day, while riding the metro to the city, Vikas struck up a conversation with a stranger seated next to him. The stranger, whose name was Emily, was a film enthusiast and mentioned that she was planning to see a new movie that evening.

Vikas, who was in the mood for a movie, asked if Emily would like some company. Emily, who was happy to have someone to share the experience with, agreed.

As they rode the metro together, Vikas and Emily chatted about their interests and shared recommendations for their favorite films. They were both excited to see the movie and were looking forward to a fun evening.

When they arrived at the theater, Vikas and Emily bought tickets and found seats in the back row. As the lights dimmed and the film began, they settled in to enjoy the show.

As the movie played on, Vikas and Emily found themselves laughing and enjoying each other's company. When the film ended, they left the theater feeling satisfied and happy.

From then on, Vikas and Emily remained friends and continued to explore the city and try new things together. And every time they rode the metro, they thought back to the chance encounter that had led to a memorable and enjoyable evening.

ZANY PERSONALITY

There was once a man named Pavan who was known for his zany personality and love of fun. He was always up for a good time and had a knack for bringing joy and laughter to those around him.

One day, while riding the metro to the city, Pavan decided to liven up the ride for his fellow passengers. He began to sing and dance in the aisles, much to the surprise and delight of his fellow riders.

As Pavan sang and danced, people couldn't help but smile and join in. Soon, the entire train was filled with laughter and joy as Pavan led the passengers in a raucous sing-along.

As they arrived at their destination, Pavan and his fellow passengers left the train feeling uplifted and happy. And as they went about their day, they couldn't help but feel grateful to have crossed paths with the crazy and fun-loving Pavan.

PASSION

There was once a film director named Gopi Krishna who was struggling with his career. Despite his talent and passion, Gopi Krishna had been unable to get any of his projects off the ground and had begun to lose hope in his dreams.

One day, while riding the metro to a meeting with a potential investor, Gopi Krishna found himself feeling particularly down and discouraged. As he sat on the train, lost in thought, a kind stranger seated next to him struck up a conversation.

The stranger, whose name was Arun, was a film critic and could tell that Gopi Krishna was feeling down. He asked Gopi Krishna about his work and listened sympathetically as Gopi Krishna shared his struggles and doubts.

Arun told Gopi Krishna that he understood how difficult it was to pursue a career in film, but encouraged him to keep trying. He reminded Gopi Krishna of the passion and drive that had led him to pursue film in the first place and encouraged him to never give up on his dreams.

Gopi Krishna was touched by Arun's words and took his advice to heart. He decided to continue fighting for his projects and eventually found success as a film director.

From then on, Gopi Krishna made a point of seeking out and listening to the advice of others, especially those who had been through similar struggles. And he always remembered the kind stranger on the metro who had helped him find his way and reignite his passion for film.

DON'T BE HESITANT

There was once a man named Prabhakar who was struggling with grief and heartbreak. His younger brother, who had been suffering from a serious illness, had recently passed away and Prabhakar was struggling to come to terms with the loss.

One day, while riding the metro to the hospital to visit his brother's grave, Prabhakar found himself seated next to a woman named Anusha. Anusha was a nurse and could tell that Prabhakar was upset. She asked if he was okay and offered to listen if he needed to talk.

Prabhakar was hesitant at first, but eventually confided in Anusha about his brother's passing and the pain he was feeling. Anusha listened sympathetically and offered Prabhakar words of comfort and support. She told him that it was natural to feel grief after losing a loved one, but that it was important to find ways to honor and remember them.

Prabhakar was touched by Anusha's kindness and the sincerity of her words. He began to see that it was possible to find ways to honor and remember his brother, even in his absence.

As they arrived at their destination, Prabhakar thanked Anusha for her support and offered to take her to his brother's grave. Anusha, who was happy to pay her respects, accepted the invitation.

As they stood at the grave together, Prabhakar felt a sense of peace and closure. He knew that he would always miss his brother, but was grateful to have found a way to honor and remember him. And he was thankful to have met Anusha, the kind nurse who had helped him find his way through his grief.

MOVIES ARE NOT JUST MOVIES

There was once a film producer named Rakshit who was struggling with a gambling addiction. Despite his success in the industry, Rakshit had a tendency to take risky bets and had lost a significant amount of money as a result.

One day, while riding the metro to a meeting with a potential investor, Rakshit found himself feeling particularly down and discouraged. He had just lost a large sum of money in a bet and was worried about how he was going to pay his debts.

As he sat on the train, lost in thought, a kind stranger seated next to him struck up a conversation. The stranger, whose name was Bhargavi, was a financial advisor and could tell that Rakshit was struggling.

Bhargavi asked Rakshit about his financial situation and listened sympathetically as he shared his struggles with gambling addiction.

She told him that it was important to seek help and to take control of his finances before it was too late.

Rakshit was touched by Bhargavi's words and took her advice to heart. He decided to seek help for his addiction and to take steps to get his finances back on track.

Thanks to Bhargavi's intervention, Rakshit was able to get the support he needed and eventually found his way out of debt. And every time he rode the metro, he thought back to the kind stranger who had helped him see the importance of seeking help and taking control of his finances.

GRANDPARENTS ARE THE BEST STORY TELLERS

Nagamani was a grandmother who lived in a small village in the countryside. She had a kind and gentle nature, and everyone in the village loved her.

One day, Nagamani decided to visit her son and daughter-in-law who lived in the city. They had recently moved to the city, and Nagamani was excited to see them and explore the city.

As she was walking through the city, Nagamani noticed that many people were riding on the metro. She had never ridden on a metro before, and she was curious about it. So, she decided to buy a ticket and hop on the metro.

As she rode the metro, Nagamani noticed that many of the passengers looked stressed and rushed. She decided to try to lighten the mood by telling them some of her favorite stories.

At first, the passengers were hesitant to listen to Nagamani, but as she told her stories with such enthusiasm and joy, they couldn't help but be drawn in. Soon, the entire car was listening to Nagamani's tales of adventure and magic.

As the metro pulled into the station, Nagamani's stories had brought a smile to everyone's face. The passengers all thanked her and told her that they looked forward to hearing more of her stories on their next ride.

Nagamani was thrilled that she had been able to bring a little bit of joy to the passengers on the metro. From then on, she made it a habit to ride the metro regularly and tell her stories to anyone who would listen.

HYDERABAD METRO TALES

There once was a writer named Hyderabad who lived in the city of Hyderabad. He was an avid traveler and loved nothing more than exploring new places and meeting new people.

One day, Hyderabad decided to take a ride on the metro. As he rode the metro, he was struck by the diverse group of people that he saw. There were young and old, rich and poor, people of all different cultures and backgrounds.

Inspired by this diversity, Hyderabad began to jot down notes in his notebook. He wrote about the different people he saw, their stories and their lives.

As he rode the Hyderabad metro, he noticed that many of the passengers were lost in their own thoughts, seemingly unaware of the world around them. He decided to try to capture the essence of the metro experience in his writing.

Over time, his notes grew into a collection of short stories that he called "Hyderabad Metro Tales." He published the stories in a small magazine, and they quickly gained a devoted following.

The stories were filled with vivid descriptions of the sights and sounds of the metro, and they captured the unique sense of community that existed among the passengers.

As the popularity of "Hyderabad Metro Tales" grew, he became known as the "writer of the metro." He continued to ride the metro regularly, always on the lookout for new stories and inspiration. And his tales of the metro continued to bring joy and connection to the riders of the metro.

MEMORIES AT CHARMINAR

There was once a writer named Sundhar who lived in the city of Hyderabad. Sundhar had a close friend named Sohan who lived in the city, but they had lost touch over the years.

One day, Sundhar received news that Sohan had passed away suddenly. Sundhar was heartbroken and couldn't believe that his dear friend was gone.

As he grieved, Sundhar remembered all the good times that he and Sohan had shared. They had always loved exploring the city and visiting new places together.

One of their favorite places to go was the Charminar, a famous monument in the city. They had spent many hours walking around the area, taking in the sights and sounds of the bustling marketplaces.

As Sundhar rode the metro, he couldn't help but think about Sohan and all the memories they had shared.

He decided to get off at the Charminar station and take a walk around the area.

As he walked, Sundhar couldn't help but feel a sense of sadness and loss. But at the same time, he also felt a sense of peace and connection to his friend. He spent hours walking around the area, remembering all the good times they had shared.

Eventually, Sundhar made his way back to the metro station and continued his journey home. But he knew that he would always carry the memories of his dear friend Sohan with him, and he vowed to visit the Charminar again in the future to remember and honor their friendship.

ACKNOWLEDGEMENT

Writing a book is harder than I thought and more rewarding than I could have ever imagined. None of this would have been possible without my parents because they supported me from the beginning and they encouraged me in every field I chose. I thank all my friends who supported me by reading my stories and sharing their opinions. I am thankful to all my friends for supporting me.

ABOUT THE AUTHOR

Tadi Vamsi Krishna

Vamsi Krishna is an author of thrillers for both adults and teens. He's passionate about writing. As a young author, he has published more than 34 stories and a few books so far. To know more about him, follow him on Instagram at @itsvamsiiiii, @ismav creative works. Email: kothakick@gmail.com and Contact No:+91 9491231566

LETTER

Dear Reader,

Let me ask you something — who is the writer without their readers? It is an eternal question — would art exist without spectator? I don't know the answer. But I know that every time I write — I write with my readers in mind. Readers are the writer's mirror — in you, we see the reflection of our words and ideas. You help us to shape them, translate thoughts into sentences and communicate them with you. Knowing that there are people who are genuinely interested in the ideas that we share makes it a whole more interesting. It creates a space for conversation - writing is not a monologue. It's an indescribable feeling to know that you've touched someone's life, maybe changed it a bit or just gave them a reminder of a thing that they've already known. Writing makes us friends with the people that we've never met and probably never will. In connects and unites us no matter where we are and who we are.

So thank you, dear reader!

www.ingramcontent.com/pod-product-compliance
Lightning Source LLC
Chambersburg PA
CBHW061432160726
47995CB00003B/856